Y0-CAE-945

SHORT TALES CLASSICS

Lewis Carroll's

Alice's Adventures in Wonderland

Down the Rabbit-Hole

Adapted by Dan Mishkin
Illustrated by Tom Mandrake

GREEN LEVEL

• Familiar topics

• Frequently used words

• Repeating language patterns

BLUE LEVEL

• New ideas introduced

• Larger vocabulary

• Variety of language patterns

PINK LEVEL

• More complex ideas

• Extended vocabulary

• Expanded sentence structures

To learn more about Short Tales leveling, go to www.abdopublishing.com

Published by Magic Wagon, a division of the ABDO Publishing Group, 8000 West 78th Street, Edina, Minnesota, 55439. Copyright © 2008 by Abdo Consulting Group, Inc. International copyrights reserved in all countries. All rights reserved. No part of this book may be reproduced in any form without written permission from the publisher. Short Tales ™ is a trademark and logo of Magic Wagon.

Printed in the United States.

Written by Lewis Carroll
Adapted Text by Dan Mishkin
Illustrations by Tom Mandrake
Colors by Wes Hartman
Edited by Stephanie Hedlund
Interior Layout by Kristen Fitzner Denton
Book Design and Packaging by Shannon Eric Denton

Library of Congress Cataloging-in-Publication Data
Mishkin, Daniel.
  Lewis Carroll's Alice's adventures in Wonderland : down the rabbit-hole / adapted by Dan Mishkin ; illustrated by Tom Mandrake.
     p. cm. -- (Short tales classics)
  ISBN 978-1-60270-119-9
 [1. Fantasy.] I. Mandrake, Tom, 1956- ill. II. Carroll, Lewis, 1832-1898. Alice's adventures in Wonderland. III. Title. IV. Title: Alice's adventures in Wonderland. V. Title: Down the rabbit-hole.
PZ7.M684325Le 2008
[E]--dc22
                          2007036968

Contents

CHAPTER ONE: THE WHITE RABBIT

Alice was tired of sitting by the river.

Her sister was reading a book. But the book had no pictures.

Alice had nothing to do. She felt bored and sleepy. Suddenly, a White Rabbit ran past her.

Alice heard it say, "Oh dear! Oh dear! I will be too late!"

Then the Rabbit took a watch out of its pocket.

He looked at it and hurried on.

Alice had never seen a rabbit with a pocket watch before.

She was very curious about it.

Alice ran across the field after the Rabbit.

It popped down a large rabbit-hole under the hedge.

She was just in time to see it go.

Alice followed the Rabbit down into the hole.

She never once thought how she would get out again.

The rabbit-hole suddenly dipped down and became a deep well.

Alice began to fall.

Down, down,
    down she went.

Alice noticed something odd. The sides of the well were filled with cupboards, bookshelves, and pictures.

Suddenly, she came down upon a heap of sticks and dry leaves. With a thump, the fall was over.

Alice was not a bit hurt.

CHAPTER TWO: THE LITTLE DOOR

Alice jumped to her feet.

She looked around and there was the White Rabbit.

He was hurrying down a long hallway.

Away like the wind, Alice ran after the Rabbit.

As it turned a corner, the Rabbit spoke. "Oh my ears and whiskers, how late it's getting!" it said.

Alice was close behind. But when she turned the corner, the Rabbit was gone.

Alice found herself in a long room.

There were doors all around the room.

But they were all locked.

Alice wondered how she was ever to get out.

Then, Alice came upon a little table with three legs.
It was made of solid glass.

There was nothing on it but a tiny golden key.

Alice thought the key might belong to one of the
doors.

But either the locks were too large or the key was too small.
The key would not open any of them.

Alice went around a second time.

She came upon a low curtain she had
not noticed before.

Behind the curtain was a little door about 15 inches high.

Alice tried the little golden key in the lock.

To her great delight it fit!

Alice knelt down and looked along the passage through the door.

She saw a lovely garden on the other side.

Alice wanted to wander among the bright flowers.

But she could not even get her head through the doorway.

Alice wished she could fold up like a telescope.

It was an odd idea.

But she had begun to think very few things were really impossible.

CHAPTER THREE: "DRINK ME" AND "EAT ME"

Alice went back to the table.

There, she saw a little bottle.

A label was tied around the neck of the bottle.

The label said "Drink Me" in large letters.

But Alice was wise.

"No, I'll look at it first," she said. She checked to make sure it didn't say "poison."

She knew not to drink something marked "poison."

The bottle was not marked "poison."

Alice decided to taste it.

She found it very nice.

It tasted like cherry pie, custard, roast turkey, and hot buttered toast mixed together.

She soon finished it.

Alice felt herself growing smaller and smaller.

"What a curious feeling," she said.

Soon, she was only ten inches high.

Alice was now the right size for going through the little door! She could enter the lovely garden.

She waited first to see if she was going to shrink any further.

When nothing more happened, she decided to go through the little door.

But Alice had forgotten the little golden key!

She went back to the table for it. But, she found she could not possibly reach it.

Alice tried her best to climb
up one of the table legs.

But it was too slippery.

She finally tired herself out
with trying.

Then, the poor little girl sat
down and cried.

"There's no use in crying like this!" she said to herself.

Then she spotted a little box. It was lying under the table.

Alice opened the box and found a very small cake.

The words "EAT ME" were beautifully marked on the cake in tiny raisins.

"Well, I'll eat it," Alice said, "and if it makes me grow larger, I can reach the key.

Alice ate a little bit, holding her hand on the top of her head.

She wanted to feel which way it was going.

Nothing happened at first.

She finished the cake.

Then she found herself growing and growing.

When she looked down at her feet they seemed almost out of sight.

Her head struck the ceiling.

Alice was now more than
nine feet high!

She was never going to
get into the lovely garden.
Alice sat down and began
to cry.